Angus
and the Cat

STORY AND PICTURES

BY

MARJORIE FLACK

SCHOLASTIC INC.

New York Toronto London Auckland Sydney

Each day as Angus grew older he grew longer but not much higher. Scottie dogs grow that way.

Now as Angus grew older and longer he learned MANY THINGS. He learned it is best to stay in one's own yard   and

ISBN: 0-590-12067-0

16 15 14 13 12 11 10 9 8   6 7 8/8

Printed in the U. S. A.   07

FROGS can jump   but

NOT to jump after them   and

BALLOONS go

POP!

Angus also learned NOT to lie on the sofa and NOT to take SOMEBODY ELSE'S food and things like that.

But there was SOMETHING outdoors Angus was very
curious about but had NEVER learned about, and that was

CATS.

The leash was TOO short.

Until one day WHAT should Angus
find INDOORS lying on the SOFA but
a strange little CAT!
Angus came closer—
The CAT sat up.
Angus
came
closer—

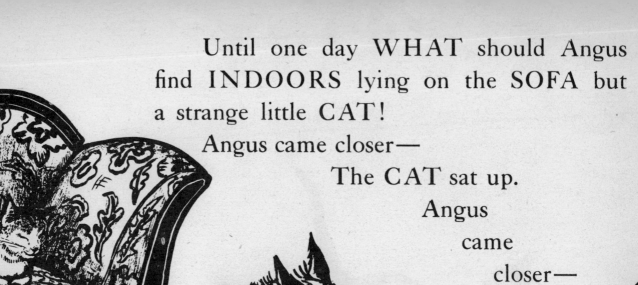

Up jumped the CAT onto the arm
of the sofa. Angus came closer and—

SISS-S-S-S-S!!!
That little CAT boxed
Angus's ears!

Woo-oo-oof—Woo-oo-oof!
said Angus.
Up jumped the CAT onto
the sofa back, up to the mantel
—and Angus was not
high enough
to reach
her!

But at lunch time down she came
to try and take Angus's food—

though not for long.

Up she jumped
onto the table,
and Angus was not
high enough
to reach
her!

At nap time there she was sitting in Angus's own special square of sunshine—

WASHING HER FACE,

though not for long.

Up she jumped onto
the windowsill,
and Angus was not
high enough
to reach
her!

For THREE whole days Angus was very busy
chasing THAT CAT, but she always went up
out of reach until on the fourth day
he chased her UP-THE-STAIRS

into the BEDROOM and she was
completely GONE!

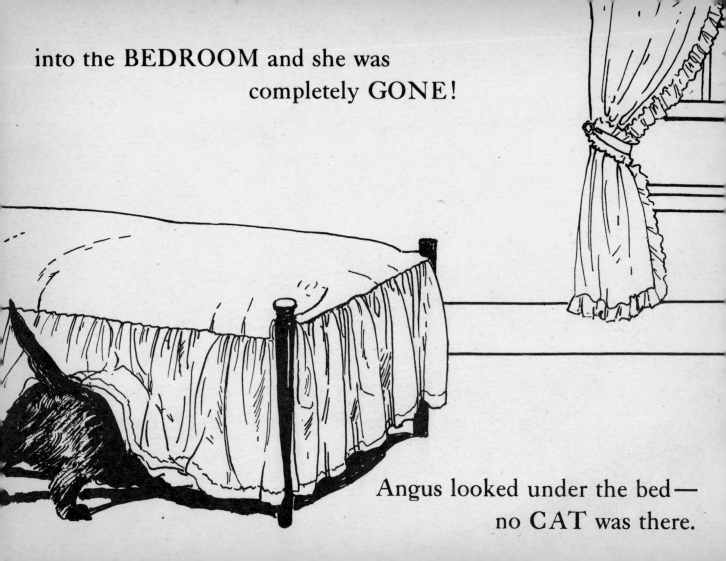

Angus looked under the bed —
no CAT was there.

Angus looked out of the window

into his yard,

into the next yard—no CAT could he see ANYWHERE.

Angus went DOWN-THE-STAIRS.
He looked on the sofa—no CAT was there.
He looked on the mantel—no CAT was there.
Angus looked on the table and

on the windowsills—

no CAT was indoors
ANYWHERE.

So Angus was ALL-ALONE. There was no CAT to box his ears. There was no CAT to take his food. There was no CAT to sit in his sunshine. There was no CAT to chase away. So Angus was ALL-ALONE and he had NOTHING-TO-DO!

Angus missed the little CAT.

But — at lunch time he heard this noise:

PURRRRR—

and there she was again.

And Angus knew

and the CAT knew

that Angus knew

that —

Angus was GLAD the cat came back!